Are you crazy about your pet?

and cuddly animals?

For budding doctors and nurses!

'I like Dr KittyCat because she helps everybody get better.'
Erin, age 5

Perfect for fans of Holly Webb.

NEWHAM LIBRARIES

9080010022 0386

'Posy the puppy is very cute and I really wanted Dr KittyCat and Peanut to help her get better.'
Aoife, age 6

'I liked the pictures because the animals were real, even though everything else was a drawing.'
Lydia, age 7

A note from the author:

Jane says . . .

'Once, my dog, Amber, had a big pink spot on her side, and she looked very, very upset. I panicked, like Peanut the mouse in this story, thinking it was a nasty injury, but it turned out to be a patch of bubble gum stuck to her fur!'

Dr KittyCat and Peanut use their vanbulance whenever they're ready to rescue. It's half ambulance and half camper van. It's also where they both sleep . . . but where? You'll have to read the story to find out!

For Amber and Bramble the
Labrados - J.C.

OXFORD
UNIVERSITY PRESS

Great Clarendon Street, Oxford OX2 6DP
Oxford University Press is a department of the University of Oxford.
It furthers the University's objective of excellence in research, scholarship,
and education by publishing worldwide in
Oxford New York
Auckland Cape Town Dar es Salaam Hong Kong Karachi
Kuala Lumpur Madrid Melbourne Mexico City Nairobi
New Delhi Shanghai Taipei Toronto
With offices in
Argentina Austria Brazil Chile Czech Republic France Greece
Guatemala Hungary Italy Japan Poland Portugal Singapore
South Korea Switzerland Thailand Turkey Ukraine Vietnam
Oxford is a registered trade mark of Oxford University Press
in the UK and in certain other countries
Text © Jane Clarke and Oxford University Press 2015
Illustrations © Oxford University Press 2015
Cover artwork: Richard Byrne
Cover photographs: Tony Campbell, Kuttelvaserova Stuchelova,
Viorel Sima/Shutterstock.com
Inside artwork: Dynamo
All animal images from Shutterstock
With thanks to Christopher Tancock for advising on the first aid
The moral rights of the author/illustrator have been asserted
Database right Oxford University Press (maker)
First published in 2015

All rights reserved. No part of this publication may be reproduced,
stored in a retrieval system, or transmitted, in any form or by any means,
without the prior permission in writing of Oxford University Press,
or as expressly permitted by law, or under terms agreed with the appropriate
reprographics rights organization. Enquiries concerning reproduction
outside the scope of the above should be sent to the Rights Department,
Oxford University Press, at the address above
You must not circulate this book in any other binding or cover
and you must impose this same condition on any acquirer

British Library Cataloguing in Publication Data
Data available
ISBN: 978-0-19-273994-0 (paperback)
2 4 6 8 10 9 7 5 3 1
Printed in China
Paper used in the production of this book is a natural, recyclable product
made from wood grown in sustainable forests. The manufacturing process
conforms to the environmental regulations of the country of origin.

Dr KittyCat

is ready to rescue

Posy the Puppy

Jane Clarke

OXFORD
UNIVERSITY PRESS

Chapter One

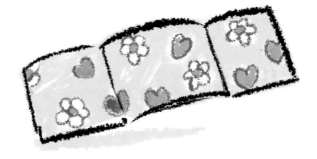

'Eek!' Peanut squeaked. 'I can't reach the sticking plasters—and Clover's ear is bleeding!'

'Don't panic, Peanut,' Dr KittyCat meowed calmly. She stretched out a paw and handed him a box of plasters from the supplies cupboard.

Peanut turned to the little bunny

next in line to see Dr KittyCat. Clover
was sobbing loudly and holding a paw
over one of his soft furry ears.

'What happened to you, Clover?'
Peanut asked.

A big fat tear rolled down the
bunny's fluffy cheek.

'I caught my ear on a bramble,'
Clover wailed. Peanut opened Dr
KittyCat's *Furry First-aid Book* and
made a quick note.

'There, there, Clover,' Dr KittyCat
meowed comfortingly, as she washed
and dried her paws. 'Now, let me see.'

Clover clamped both paws over his
ear and cried even more.

'Dr KittyCat does need to look at your sore ear,' Peanut told him gently, 'so she can make it better.'

Very slowly, Clover took his paws away from his ear. Peanut handed him a tissue and helped him wipe away his tears.

Dr KittyCat gently examined the small scrape on the bunny's ear. 'The cut's not very deep,' she murmured. 'It will heal  quickly. But first, we must clean it up.'

'I know exactly what we need. A bowl of warm water, soap, and clean cotton gauze swabs.' Peanut raced around the clinic collecting things.

'Thanks, Peanut,' Dr KittyCat smiled. 'You're a purr-fect assistant!'

Peanut whiffled through his whiskers happily as he watched Dr KittyCat treat the cut on Clover's ear.

Dr KittyCat worked calmly and steadily.
She trickled clean water over the cut,
then gently sponged away the dirt
around it, taking care to wipe away from
the wound and use a clean piece of
cotton gauze each time.

'You *are* a brave bunny,' she told Clover as she patted his ear dry.

Peanut took the bowl and the used swabs away.

'Almost done,' Dr KittyCat announced. 'It's time to put on a nice clean dressing.'

Peanut showed the little rabbit the box of sticking plasters. 'Which one would you like?' he asked.

'That one!' Clover pointed to a big square plaster decorated with sparkly stars.

'Try not to touch it,' Dr KittyCat told Clover as she carefully stuck it on. 'Your ear will heal by itself in a few days.'

'It feels fine now!' Clover
announced, giving a tiny bunny hop.
'Well done,' Peanut squeaked. 'You
can have a special reward sticker!'

He handed Clover a round sticker that said: 'I was a purr-fect patient for Dr KittyCat!'

I was a purr-fect patient for Dr KittyCat!

The young rabbit stuck it on his jumper and beamed with pride.

'Take care,' Peanut and Dr KittyCat called after Clover as he skipped out of the clinic with his cotton tail bouncing behind him.

Peanut poked his head round the door.

'There's still a long queue of little animals waiting to see us,' he told Dr KittyCat. 'They all have bumps, scrapes, and bruises.'

Dr KittyCat looked puzzled. 'Why are there are so many injuries today?' she asked.

'It's their Paws and Prizes sports day tomorrow,' Peanut reminded her, 'and some of the little ones have been practising a bit too hard.'

'Of course!' Dr KittyCat exclaimed. 'Posy told us all about it when she came in for her well puppy check-up yesterday. She's hoping to win a prize.' Dr KittyCat giggled. 'She was so excited, she raced round and round the clinic.'

'Posy's the bounciest puppy I've ever seen,' Peanut agreed. 'I was amazed you managed to do her health check. I couldn't even get her to stand still.'

He opened the door to Dr KittyCat's clinic. 'Come in, Nutmeg,' he told a small guinea pig. 'You're next . . .'

The guinea pig limped inside.

'What happened to you?' Peanut asked.

'I hurt my ankle!' the guinea pig squealed.

'There, there, Nutmeg . . .' Dr KittyCat meowed kindly.

At last, everyone had been seen.

'What a busy day!' Peanut squeaked. 'There are lots of notes to write up before we leave.' He took the *Furry First-aid Book* across to his desk.

'I'll make a start on my knitting,' Dr KittyCat said. 'I found a pattern for a purr-fectly lovely hat.'

Oh no! Peanut thought. *Please don't let it be for me.* He already had lots of things that Dr KittyCat had knitted for him and he wasn't sure he liked any of them very much.

Dr KittyCat reached into her flowery doctor's bag. 'That's odd,' she meowed. 'My bag wasn't closed properly—and I can't find the wool. I know I put it in here.'

'Maybe it rolled out and got lost,' Peanut said hopefully, as Dr KittyCat carefully checked the contents of her bag. 'Scissors, syringe, medicines, ointments, instant cool packs, paw-cleansing gel, and wipes,' she murmured.

'Stethoscope, ophthalmoscope, thermometer, tweezers, bandages, gauze, sticking plasters, and reward stickers. Everything is where it should be, except for my ball of wool . . .'

The telephone on Peanut's desk began to ring. Peanut picked up the handset.

Brring!

Brring!

'Dr KittyCat's clinic. How can we help you?' Peanut asked, twirling the telephone cord so it curled tightly round his paw.

'Just a moment . . .'

Peanut shook his paw out of the cord, and placed it over the mouthpiece.

'There's been an accident on the playing field,' Peanut squeaked. 'Posy's stuck in a tunnel on the agility course and they think she's hurt!'

'Is the vanbulance ready?' Dr KittyCat jumped to her feet.

Peanut nodded and held out the phone for her to take.

'It's such a shame,' Peanut murmured. 'Posy was so looking forward to taking part in sports day.'

Dr KittyCat took the phone.

'Keep Posy still and calm,' she meowed. 'We'll be there in a whisker!'

Chapter Two

'Don't forget your bag!' Peanut clicked the flowery doctor's bag shut and thrust it into Dr KittyCat's paws as they hurried out of the door.

The vanbulance was parked next to the clinic, looking friendly and cheerful, Peanut thought, thanks to the bright flowers he had painted on it.

He hopped into the passenger seat, carefully pulled in his tail, and shut the door. He clicked on his seatbelt, then slammed his paw against a button on the dashboard to make the light flash on top of the van.

'Ready to rescue?' he squeaked, raising his voice above the siren.

Dr KittyCat slammed her door shut, checked the mirrors and took off the brake. 'Ready to rescue!' she meowed.

Nee-nah, nee-nah, nee-nah.

The vanbulance sped through Thistletown. Peanut held tight to his seatbelt as

they bumped over the timber bridge.
Dr KittyCat was driving so fast it made
his tail bounce up and down and his
whiskers quiver and shake.

'Eek!' he squealed as they rounded
Duckpond Bend.

Dr KittyCat held tight to the big
steering wheel. 'Don't panic, Peanut,'
she meowed, putting her paw on the
accelerator. The vanbulance shook and
rattled as they went faster and faster.
'We're almost there.'

Peanut shut his eyes.

There was a *scr-ee-eech* of brakes
as Dr KittyCat parked the vanbulance
beside the playing field.

Peanut leaped out. At the far corner of the field there was an agility course with a see-saw, weave poles, a balance beam, and a high jump. A few little animals were gathered around the canvas agility tunnel. Dr KittyCat grabbed her flowery doctor's bag and hurried towards it. Peanut raced after her. As he got closer, he could hear a loud whimpering noise coming from inside the narrow tunnel.

Eew, eew, eew!

Peanut and Dr KittyCat peered into the opposite ends of the tunnel.

'I can't see anything,' Peanut exclaimed. 'Is Posy still in there?'

he asked the group of young animals.

Sage the owlet shook her feathers.
'Yes,' she hooted. 'Posy's stuck in the
bend in the middle and she won't
come out!'

Peanut raced round to the bend
in the tunnel and pressed his whiskers
against the canvas.

'Don't fret, Posy,' he squeaked. 'Dr KittyCat is here. How are you doing?'

Inside the tunnel, he could hear Posy take a deep breath.

'Aooo!' she howled. 'It hurts!'

'Oooh!' the group of little bystanders gasped.

Dr KittyCat hurried over to where Peanut was standing. 'Posy,' she meowed. 'Can you tell me where it hurts?'

There was a pause, and a lot of puppy snuffling.

'It . . . it's my leg,' Posy whimpered.

Dr KittyCat pricked up her ears. 'Posy should stay where she is until we work out what's wrong with her leg,' she whispered to Peanut. 'But I'm not sure there will be enough room for me to examine her inside the tunnel.'

'I'll go in and keep her calm while we both figure out the best way to treat her and get her out,' Peanut suggested.

'Good idea,' said Dr KittyCat. 'Take a cool pack with you.' She opened her flowery doctor's bag.

'Oooh!' The curious crowd pushed forward to get a better look.

Peanut scurried into the tunnel. There was just enough sunlight shining through

the tough canvas for him to make out
a bundle of quivering golden fur. The
fluffy little puppy was curled up in a
tight ball in the gloom.

'I'm here now, Posy,' he murmured.

A rubbery nose poked out of the
fur ball 'Ow!' she yelped.

'Posy,' Dr KittyCat meowed from outside the tunnel, 'how did you hurt yourself?'

Peanut looked at Posy. She shook her head.

'She's not sure,' Peanut squeaked. 'Maybe her friends know.'

'Did any of you see what happened?' Dr KittyCat asked them. 'Did Posy fall off the balance beam, or the see-saw?'

There was a moment's silence.

'No,' Sage hooted. 'I was watching all the time and I didn't see her fall. She just started limping and saying that she wouldn't be able to take part in Paws and Prizes tomorrow.'

'That's right,' Fennel the fox cub yipped.

'Right!' the other little animals chorused.

'How badly was she limping?' asked Dr KittyCat. 'Did she put any weight on her bad leg at all?'

'She could walk on it a bit,' Fennel yipped. Peanut watched the shadow of Sage's head bob up and down as she nodded in agreement.

'Good,' Dr KittyCat meowed. 'It doesn't sound as if Posy has broken her leg.'

'Which leg is it?' Peanut asked Posy.

'This . . . this . . . one,' the puppy moaned, stretching out one of her back legs. 'No, I mean this one.' She nuzzled one of her front legs. 'Ow!' she yelped.

'Posy can move her leg,' Peanut reported, 'but it seems to hurt at the joint.'

'It might be a sprain. That can be very painful. Put the cool pack on her leg,' Dr KittyCat instructed.

Peanut shook and squeezed the pack to make it work.

'This will help,' he said to Posy.

The tip of Posy's tail gave a tiny wag.

'You're doing very well,' Peanut said reassuringly as he held the cool pack against Posy's leg.

Outside the tunnel, he could hear a bit of a commotion.

'I'll bite it open,' Fennel suggested.

'You'll break your teeth,' Sage hooted. 'I'll peck it open.'

'You'll break your beak,' Fennel yipped.

'I'll scratch it open with my claws,' squeaked a little voice that Peanut recognized as Pumpkin the hamster.

'You'll break your claws!' Sage and Fennel said together.

'I have a better idea,' Dr KittyCat meowed. Peanut looked up as her shadow fell across the canvas tunnel. He could make out her opening her flowery doctor's bag and taking something out of it. She held up what looked like an enormous pair of shadowy scissors.

Aooo!

An excited ripple went round the group of little animals who were watching. 'Oooh!'

'She's taken out her special scissors!' Peanut squeaked excitedly. 'It's *Operation Posy!*'

'Aooo!' howled the anxious puppy.

Chapter Three

'Don't worry, Posy, I didn't mean an operation on *you!*' Peanut said. 'Her special tough-cut scissors are for helping her get to her patients.' He stared at the canvas walls of the tunnel. He could make out the shadowy outline of Dr KittyCat as she held up her scissors.

'Peanut and Posy, I'll begin at

ground level and cut up the seam,' Dr KittyCat called to them. 'Ready?'

Peanut looked at Posy. She nodded slowly.

'You're being very brave,' he murmured. 'We're ready!' he squeaked.

Dr KittyCat began to snip slowly and very carefully through the canvas.

'Do any of you know which leg Posy has hurt?' Dr KittyCat asked.

'Her front leg,' Pumpkin squeaked.

'No, it was her back leg,' said Sage.

'Well, I definitely saw her limping on her front leg when she went across the balance beam,' Pumpkin repeated.

Sage ruffled her feathers. 'Posy was definitely limping on her back leg when she went across the see-saw,' she told Dr KittyCat.

'That's odd,' Dr KittyCat murmured

as she slowly snipped her way through the seam of the canvas tunnel.

Very odd, thought Peanut.

Inside the tunnel, Posy shuffled uncomfortably. 'Ow!' she moaned.

'You'll be out soon,' Peanut consoled her. 'Try to stay still for just a little bit longer . . .'

Outside the tunnel, he could hear Dr KittyCat asking more questions.

'Did anyone else notice anything wrong with Posy?' she meowed.

'I did!' quacked a duckling.

'That's my best friend, Willow!' Posy yapped. She pricked up her ears as Willow talked to Dr KittyCat.

'Posy was upset when she was standing on the start line,' Willow quacked. 'I heard her whimper.'

'So did Posy start whimpering before she started limping?' Dr KittyCat meowed.

'I think so,' Willow explained.

'She set off really slowly, too. She's usually ever so fast.'

'Yesterday, she told me she was fast enough to win a medal,' Dr KittyCat murmured. 'Something must have been wrong before the start . . .'

Posy fidgeted uncomfortably.

Peanut patted her paw. 'Try to keep still,' he squeaked.

'Poor Posy,' Sage hooted. 'She really wants to win a medal at Paws and Prizes tomorrow, but I don't suppose she can now . . .'

'Eew, eew, eew,' Posy whimpered.

'I'll be there in a whisker, Posy!' Dr KittyCat made a last snip with her tough-cut scissors, and pulled back the canvas. Peanut blinked in the flood of bright sunlight.

Posy uncurled her head and stuck her little muzzle into the air.

'Aooo!' she howled.

'We'll make you feel better very soon, Posy,' Dr KittyCat meowed softly. She put the tough-cut scissors back in her flowery doctor's bag and snapped it shut, then turned to Posy's friends.

'Willow, Fennel, Pumpkin, and Sage . . . thank you very much, you've been a great help,' she told them. 'But now, I need you to stand back to give us some space while we take care of Posy.'

The young animals backed off a little way.

'Posy,' Dr KittyCat meowed. 'I need to take a proper look so I can find out what's wrong, and fix it. Are you ready?'

Posy slowly nodded her head.

'It's a bit of a puzzle,' Dr KittyCat whispered to Peanut, 'but we'll work it out.'

Peanut nodded. 'Sometimes being a doctor is just like being a detective!' he squeaked, as he carefully lifted the cool pack away from the poorly puppy's leg.

Chapter Four

'You are a brave puppy,' Dr KittyCat
purred gently as she carefully examined
Posy's leg.

'Her leg doesn't look swollen,'
Peanut commented.

Dr KittyCat gently placed her
furry paws on Posy's leg. 'It doesn't
feel lumpy or hot, either,' she agreed.

'Can you wiggle your toes, Posy?'

Posy wriggled all her toes.

'That's very good.' Dr KittyCat smiled.

Posy slowly lifted her head. 'It hurts,' she whimpered.

'There, there, Posy,' Peanut murmured. 'Dr KittyCat will find out what the problem is.'

Dr KittyCat nodded and took hold of Posy's paw. She bent her head to Peanut's level.

'We must check to see if Posy has any other worrying symptoms,' she whispered to Peanut. 'She might be suffering from shock.'

'The first signs of shock are a quick pulse and cold skin,' Peanut squeaked quietly into Dr KittyCat's furry ear. 'And Posy is a bit shivery . . .'

Dr KittyCat nodded.

'I'm going to check your heart beat,' she told Posy as she held her paw on the pulse point on Posy's wrist.

'That's excellent, Posy!' Dr KittyCat purred calmly. 'Your heart is beating strongly and regularly. You're not in shock.'

Peanut sighed with relief. 'She must have been shivery because of the cold pack!' he squeaked.

'Now I'll check your breathing,' Dr KittyCat told Posy. 'Pass me my stethoscope, please, Peanut.'

Peanut very carefully pulled it out of the bag. Dr KittyCat always made sure that she had her stethoscope with her, and she often used it to check her patients' lungs.

Dr KittyCat popped in the earpieces and pressed the disc against Posy's chest.

'Everything sounds good,' she told Posy. 'Your breathing is fine. Not too deep and not too shallow, no rattling noises . . .'

She turned to Peanut. 'All Posy's vital signs are good. She's doing very well. Just one more check before

we can allow her to move. I want to
take a good look at her eyes to make
sure she won't get dizzy. Pass me the
ophthalmoscope, Peanut.'

Peanut took out something the size
and shape of a small torch.

'This is a special doctor's instrument for checking eyes,' Dr KittyCat explained to Posy as she held it close to the puppy's tear-filled eyes.

'That's perfect, Posy,' she said. 'Well done! You've passed all the tests and you can sit up now if you feel well enough.'

The little puppy slowly sat up. Her ears drooped. 'Eew, eew, eew!' she yelped.

'This is all very odd,' Dr KittyCat said thoughtfully. She swished her stripy tail. 'I can't find anything wrong with Posy's leg,' she told Peanut. 'But she's still whimpering . . .'

'Her tail has lost its wag, too,' Peanut squeaked, looking at the dejected puppy. 'I wonder if she's telling us the truth about her leg . . .' he whispered.

Dr KittyCat's ears pricked up. She blinked her bright eyes.

'We're a bit puzzled, Posy,' Dr KittyCat meowed. 'Does it hurt anywhere else?'

Posy raised her little muzzle to the sky.

'Aooo!' she howled. 'Here!' And she began to rub her tummy with her paw.

'You *are* a good puppy for telling us,' Dr KittyCat said. She turned to Peanut. 'Is there anything in your notes about Posy ever having tummy ache?' she asked.

Peanut flipped open the *Furry First-aid Book*. He quickly read through the sections that referred to Posy.

'There's no mention of a poorly tummy,' he murmured. 'And we know that Posy was fine and frisky when she came to the clinic yesterday.'

'She certainly was,' Dr KittyCat meowed. 'Bouncing everywhere, knocking over my bag, and even leaving chew marks on the table leg with her pointy puppy teeth!'

'Chew marks!' Peanut exclaimed. 'Of course! Puppies love to chew. It must be something she's eaten. Posy! Have you swallowed or chewed up anything you shouldn't have?' he squeaked.

Posy hung her head and looked at the ground.

'You can tell us,' Peanut said encouragingly. 'We won't be cross.'

Posy gave a big sniff. 'I don't really have a bad leg,' she confessed. 'And I'm sorry for not telling the truth . . . but I didnt want to get into trouble.'

Peanut and Dr KittyCat looked at one another.

'We promise you won't get into trouble,' Peanut reassured Posy. 'It's really important you tell us what you did that made you feel so poorly.'

'I . . . I knocked over Dr KittyCat's flowery doctor's bag,' Posy told them.

'That didn't make you feel poorly, did it?' Peanut asked, puzzled.

'No . . . but then I nibbled at something,' Posy groaned. 'It was only a little nibble . . . but now I feel too sick to take part in Paws and Prizes.' She gave a big sob.

'What did you nibble, Posy?' Peanut prompted her.

Posy's ears drooped so low they dragged on the ground. 'I took a little nibble of something that rolled out of Dr KittyCat's flowery doctor's bag,' she whimpered.

Peanut gasped. 'Eek!' he squeaked. 'What if she's eaten some of your pills,

Dr KittyCat? That's really dangerous! She could be poisoned! I should have locked your bag away safely!'

'Don't panic, Peanut,' said Dr KittyCat calmly. 'All the pills are in puppy-proof containers, and none of my medicines are missing.'

She turned to the little puppy.

'We're not cross with you, Posy. But we do need to know what rolled out of my bag and what you took a little nibble of.'

'It was a bit more than a nibble,' Posy sniffed.

'That's OK,' Dr KittyCat purred. 'You can tell me.'

'I . . . I chewed up one of your things!' Posy lifted her head and looked Dr KittyCat in the eye. 'I tried to spit it out, but I couldn't—and I couldn't swallow it, either. I haven't been able to eat anything since then, and I'm *so* hungry . . .'

'Hunger pangs can be very painful,' Peanut said sympathetically. 'That would explain why your tummy hurts.'

'We need to check out why you can't swallow,' Dr KittyCat meowed. 'I'll have to look down your throat, Posy. Open wide . . .'

Posy opened her jaws to show two rows of tiny sharp teeth and a big pink tongue. 'I will have to push your tongue down, so that I can see properly,' Dr KittyCat murmured. Peanut handed her the tongue compressor and Dr KittyCat pressed it down carefully on Posy's tongue.

'There's something stuck at the back of Posy's throat . . .' Dr KittyCat said slowly. 'Take a look, Peanut.'

Peanut peered into Posy's mouth. 'I can see it!' Peanut squeaked excitedly. 'I can see what the matter is!'

Chapter Five

At the back of Posy's throat, Peanut could make out a small soggy wodge of something stringy.

'It's your knitting wool!' Peanut squeaked.

'So that's where it got to!' Dr KittyCat meowed. 'Now we know what's wrong! You have some wool stuck at the back of your throat,' she told Posy. 'No wonder you're feeling poorly. Can you give a really big cough?'

Ak . . . aak . . . aaak! Posy coughed. The spitty wad of wool shot out onto the ground.

'Well done!' Peanut and Dr KittyCat exclaimed together.

Woof! Posy leaped to her feet, wagging her tail.

Her friends hurried back over. 'Yay!' they cheered.

'Posy is feeling better already,' Peanut said.

'She'll be fine. We just need to keep an
eye on her for a little while. She'll see
you later.'

'Bye, Posy!' Willow quacked.
'Get well soon!'

Peanut led the way to the
vanbulance.

'I've never seen inside, before,' Posy
yapped excitedly.

'You'll love it!' Peanut said. 'We do!'
He slid the side door of the van open.

'Wow!' Posy woofed. 'It's got flowery curtains and cushions and everything!'

Peanut settled Posy on the bench

seat beside the table. He tucked a
blanket around her. In a moment,
little puppy snores echoed round
the vanbulance.

'I feel much better,' Posy yawned when
she woke from her nap. 'I should go back
home now, before anyone gets worried.'

'Remember to be careful about what you chew and swallow,' Peanut told her as he slid open the door.

'I will,' Posy promised. She paused at the door. 'I can take part in Paws and Prizes tomorrow, can't I?'

'Of course!' Peanut and Dr KittyCat said together.

Posy yapped for joy. Then, suddenly, her ears and tail drooped.

'You're not feeling poorly again, are you?' Peanut squeaked worriedly.

'The tunnel,' Posy howled. 'It's ruined because of me. There can't be an agility course without an agility tunnel. I've spoilt the whole day for everyone!'

'I've already thought of that,' Peanut grinned. 'It's nothing that a mouse with a needle and some surgical thread can't mend! I keep an emergency supply in the van.'

'Yay!' Posy jumped up and down, wagging her tail. 'Will you come and watch me tomorrow?' she asked. 'Pleeease?'

'Yes!' Dr KittyCat laughed. 'We'll be here anyway—we're providing the first aid!

In fact,' she meowed, 'we might as well stay here tonight.'

Posy's eyes opened wide as she looked around the vanbulance. 'But where do you sleep?' she asked. 'I can't see any beds.'

'The table folds away and then this bench turns into a bed for Dr KittyCat,' Peanut explained. 'And I have my very own room, up here.' He scrambled up to a little cabin built into the roof and waved down at Posy. 'I have my own bed and desk and chair and everything!'

'Cool! Thanks for showing me,' Posy yapped as she waved goodbye. 'I wish I could live in a vanbulance!'

Chapter Six

It was the morning of Paws and Prizes, and Peanut was up early to mend the agility tunnel.

'It looks as good as new!' said Dr KittyCat, admiring Peanut's row of tiny, neat stitches in the canvas. 'You'd make a very good surgeon, Peanut.'

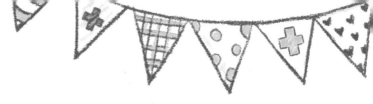

Peanut's tail twitched happily as he gathered up his needle and thread. 'We better get out of the way,' he squeaked. 'The competitions start soon.'

Dr KittyCat and Peanut made their way back to the vanbulance. Peanut set up the Furry First-aid sign and Dr KittyCat put her flowery doctor's bag beside it. They each fetched a folding chair from the vanbulance.

'It's a lovely sunny day,' Dr KittyCat sighed, 'and no-one has needed first aid yet.' Then she winked at Peanut and said, 'It would have been the perfect moment to do some knitting if my wool wasn't so soggy!'

Peanut picked up his pencil, opened the *Furry First-aid Book* and began to write up the notes he had made about Posy. 'You did very well to work out what was wrong with Posy,' he told Dr KittyCat. 'It was a difficult case.'

'Very tricky,' Dr KittyCat agreed. 'I couldn't have done it without your help, Peanut.'

Peanut grinned such a big grin that his whiskers whiffled.

Just then, a big cheer echoed across the playing field. Peanut and Dr KittyCat looked up.

'Posy's about to start the agility competition,' Dr KittyCat said, smiling.

'I hardly dare look,' Peanut squeaked as Posy tip-toed along the balance beam, raced up and down the see-saw, and dashed in and out of the weave poles. She squirmed through the mended tunnel and leaped over the high jump.

Even from a distance they could hear her excited yap-yap-yaps as she raced across the finish line.

'Phew!' Peanut put his nose back in his notes. 'She didn't hurt herself, and she made good time. She might even get a rosette.'

'We'll have to wait and see,' purred Dr KittyCat.

Half an hour later, the loudspeaker crackled into life. 'Congratulations to everyone who took part in the agility competition,' it announced. 'The winners are . . . in third place, Fennel! In second place, Posy! And in first place, Nutmeg! We invite Dr KittyCat and Peanut to present the rosettes.'

'That's us!' Peanut snapped the first-aid book shut and Dr KittyCat stood up and stowed her flowery doctor's bag safely in the vanbulance. Then they hurried to the podium where the winners were waiting. Posy was standing there proudly, wagging her tail so hard it was a blur.

Peanut passed Dr KittyCat the rosettes and she presented them to the winners. Then, as Dr KittyCat and Peanut were leaving the podium, Posy ran after them.

'Thank you,' she yapped, proudly patting her rosette with her paw.

'I won this rosette because you made me better!'

'You're welcome, Posy!' Dr KittyCat meowed.

'I'm hoping to get another rosette, too,' Posy whispered to Peanut.

The loudspeaker crackled again. 'The next race is the sack race,' it announced.

'Yippee!' Posy squealed, bouncing up and down on all fours.

Dr KittyCat and Peanut stood back,
as a crowd of over-excited puppies
and kittens raced to the start line and
wriggled into the sacks.

'Ready . . . steady . . . go!' boomed
the voice from the loudspeaker.

There was an eruption of squeals,

squeaks, and howls as the little animals
bumped and tripped and crashed into
each other.

'Dr KittyCat and Peanut are
needed at the first-aid post,' said the
loudspeaker voice.

'Uh-oh!' squeaked Peanut.

A long line of animals with minor bumps, bruises, and cuts was waiting at the vanbulance.

'We would like to thank Dr KittyCat and Peanut for providing our first aid today,' the announcer went on. 'They make a great team.'

Peanut and Dr KittyCat grinned at
each other.

'We do,' Dr KittyCat meowed,
as she took her flowery doctor's bag
out of the vanbulance and put it
down beside her. 'Pass me the sticking
plasters, Peanut!'

The end

What's in Dr KittyCat's bag?

Here are just some of the things that Dr KittyCat always carries in her flowery doctor's bag.

Tough-cut scissors

These special scissors are strong but not sharp! Dr KittyCat uses them in first-aid emergencies to cut through clothing or other materials without harming her patients. She also uses them for cutting bandages and plasters.

Stethoscope

With a stethoscope, Dr KittyCat can listen to sounds from inside her patients' bodies. At the end of the stethoscope there is a rounded 'bell' side and a flatter 'diaphragm' side and each side is used

for listening to different sounds,
such as a heartbeat or the sound
of breathing.

Cool pack

Dr KittyCat always makes
sure she has enough cool
packs in her bag. She uses
each pack only once by squeezing
it gently so that it quickly becomes
cold enough to soothe bumps,
bruises, strains, and sprains.

Tongue depressor

Peanut thinks tongue
depressors look like ice-lolly sticks!
But in fact Dr KittyCat uses these
flat, thin, rounded wooden blades to
gently press down a patient's tongue
so that she can have a better view of
their mouth and throat.

If you loved Posy the Puppy, here's an extract
from another Dr KittyCat adventure:

Dr KittyCat is ready to rescue:
Clover the Bunny

This time Dr KittyCat is helping a bunny called
Clover whose paws get covered in tiny little
spots during a camping trip . . .

Dr KittyCat, Nutmeg, Pumpkin, and Peanut raced towards Clover's cries. At the far side, there was a pile of wood near the base of an old tree trunk.

'He dropped his firewood,' Pumpkin said, worriedly. 'Something must have happened to him!'

'Waah!' Clover wailed again. Dr KittyCat's ears pricked up. Peanut glanced round wildly, but all he could see was shadows.

Here are some other stories that we think you'll love!

MICHAEL BOND
CREATOR OF PADDINGTON BEAR

The Tales of
Olga da Polga

A little guinea-pig and her big adventures!

ILLUSTRATED BY
CATHERINE RAYNER

ASTRID LINDGREN
much-loved author of *Pippi Longstocking*

LOTTA MAKES A MESS!

The **Tree House**
a whole new world of adventure ...

Gillian Cross
Winner of the *Smarties Prize*

ANNE BOOTH

Can Lucy make Starlight better and save Christmas?

Lucy's Secret REINDEER

'I've spotted him!' Dr KittyCat exclaimed. She pointed to a little mound of fur huddled up in the dappled light. It was Clover, quivering from his whiskery nose to his cotton-wool tail.

'Waah!' Clover cried. 'Waah!'

'Dr KittyCat's come to rescue you, Clover,' Peanut squeaked. 'Everything will be all right now.'